The

ORPHAN SEAL

With warmest thanks to the staff and volunteers at the
New England Aquarium's Animal Care Center for their invaluable
help, and in memory of John H. Prescott, former executive director,
who established the marine animal rescue program.

—*FH and DP*

Story copyright © 2000 by Fran Hodgkins
Illustrations copyright © 2000 by Dawn Peterson

Printed in China

DownEastBooks
www.nbnbooks.com
Distributed by
National Book Network
800-462-6420

Manufacturer's Information
1010 Printing International Limited
Yuanzhou, China
June 2013

ISBN 978-0-89272-471-0

Library of Congress Catalog Card Number 99-59578

The
ORPHAN SEAL

By Fran Hodgkins

Illustrated by Dawn Peterson

Down East Books

The storm is over, but waves still pound the beach on the coast of Maine. A tiny seal pup struggles to pull himself out of the surf. The waves crash around him, trying to drag him back into the sea. He's just a few days old, and he is lost. The storm's waves pulled him away from his mother and tossed him head over tail through the water. They could not find each other. And that's a problem, because this pup is too young to survive on his own. He still needs his mother's milk, just as you did when you were a baby. And he needs her to teach him how to hunt for fish and escape enemies.

With one last effort, the pup frees himself from the water's grip. Safe beyond the sea's reach, he pauses and looks around. The weak, late afternoon sun barely pierces the heavy clouds. The pup blinks sand from his big, black eyes.

"Ohhh-roooo!" he calls.

The beach is empty. His mother doesn't answer. Weary from all his hard swimming, the pup closes his eyes for a nap.

The pup isn't actually alone. On a rock nearby sit a man and a boy. They saw the little lost seal come out of the water. They have called the New England Aquarium in Boston, Massachusetts. The scientist there, Greg Early, told them to watch the pup.

"If a day goes by and the pup's mother does not return, I'll come to Maine, get the pup, and bring him back here to the aquarium," he said.

Because the little seal, like all marine mammals, is protected by law, only certain licensed people can go near him to help. Greg is one of those people.

Night comes. The pup sleeps very little. Whenever he wakes, he calls his mother again. By daybreak, the pup gives up.

At the same time, a hundred and fifty miles south in Boston, Connie, the supervisor of the seal rescue program, helps Greg pack their truck, and the two set off for Maine. As part of their work for the aquarium, they rescue, take care of, and release sea animals that are hurt or too sick to look out for themselves, and so have come ashore or become stranded. They and the rest of the staff at the aquarium's special hospital have helped sea turtles, whales, dolphins, and many, many seals. Most of these are harbor seals, the most common kind along the New England coast.

It is April. At this time of year, the center gets lots of calls about baby seals, because female harbor seals give birth in the spring. Many pups show up on beaches, but not all of them are in trouble. Just like you, they can get chilled in the early-spring ocean, so they come onto the beach to warm up. They aren't alone. Mom is usually in the water nearby, keeping an eye on her baby.

Seal mothers are usually very good at watching over their pups. But if a storm hits, the waves may toss the mother one way and the baby seal another. That's what happened to the pup in Maine.

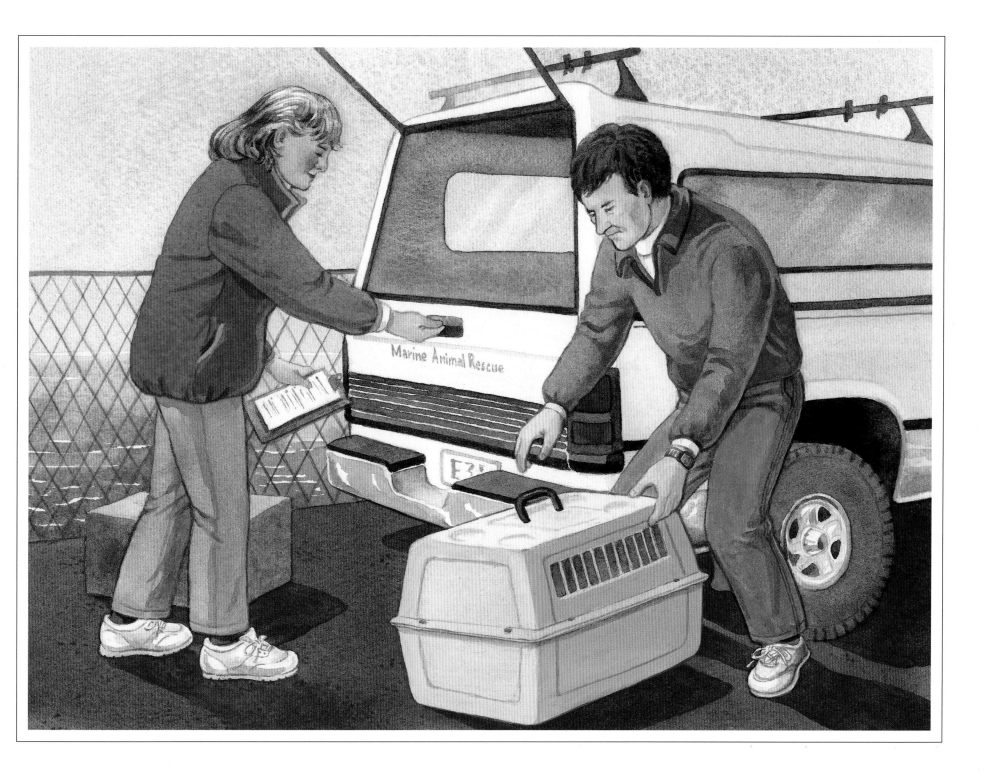

Other mother seals have a different problem. Their pups may have been born sick or too early. If that had happened to you, you would have stayed in a hospital until you were strong enough to go home. But in the wild, a seal needs to be healthy so it can escape dangers like sharks and speeding boats. By staying with a sick pup that is too weak to swim well, the mother seal puts her own life in danger. So even though she doesn't want to, sometimes she has to leave her baby.

It is mid-morning on the beach in Maine, and Greg and Connie have arrived. They have watched the baby seal for half an hour, so they know that the pup's mother is nowhere to be found. They get ready to take him back to Boston.

As Connie gets the carrier out of the truck, Greg approaches the pup quietly and carefully. Although the little seal may look like a cuddly toy, he is a wild animal. His teeth are small, but sharp, and he could bite if frightened. Greg never forgets that.

The pup watches the man come near. He is weak from hunger and chilled from the night on the beach. He does not run away. He just squirms a little as Greg picks him up. Connie opens the wire door of the tan plastic pet carrier, and her partner gently slides the baby seal inside. The pup is too tired, cold, and hungry to struggle.

Exhausted, he falls asleep in the quiet, dark carrier as the truck heads back to Boston.

As soon as he arrives at the New England Aquarium, the pup gets a medical checkup. This lets the staff know what kind of medicine to give him to make him feel better. The aquarium veterinarian, Dr. Andy Stamper, listens to the pup's heart and lungs with a stethoscope. The pup wheezes a little when he breathes, so the vet knows he has a cold, maybe even pneumonia. With a hypodermic needle the vet takes a blood sample; by studying it under a microscope, the vet can see if the pup has any parasites.

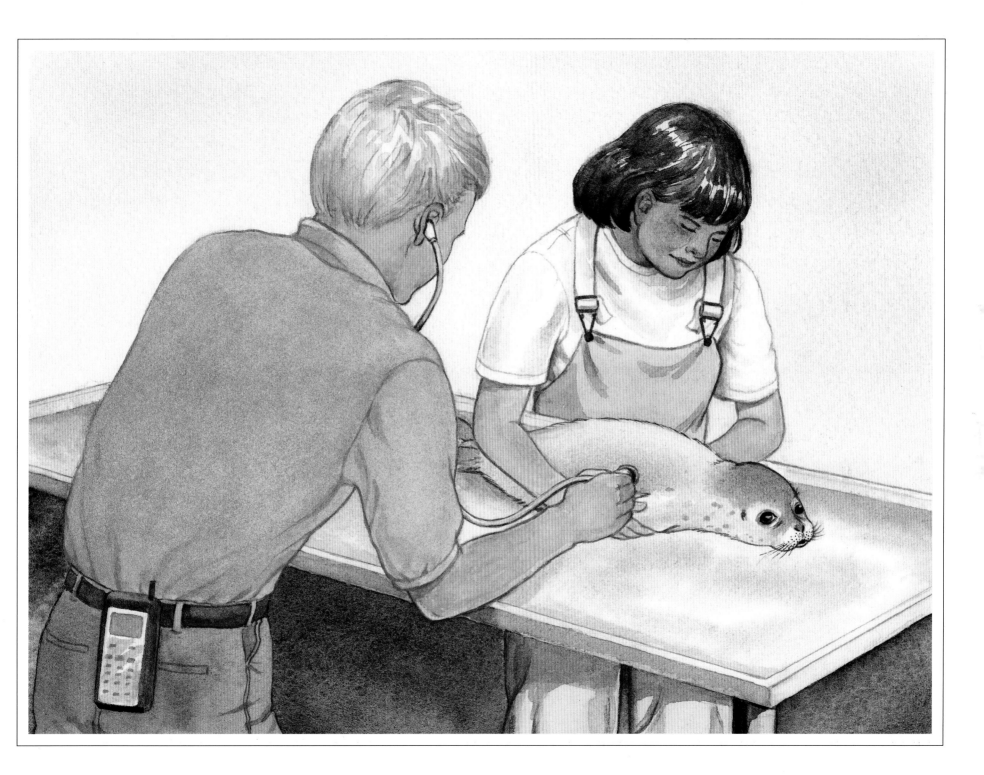

Parasites are tiny creatures that live inside bigger ones, getting their nourishment from the food the other animal eats. Healthy wild animals can handle having a few parasites. But parasites can take away the food a sick baby animal needs to get better, making it even sicker. If this seal pup has parasites, Dr. Andy can give him medicine to get rid of them. When the needle goes in, the pup complains loudly.

"Oooohhh-awwww-awwww-awwwwwh!"

When the checkup is over, Jim, an animal-care technician at the aquarium, uses rubber cement to glue a red plastic disk with the number **5** onto the pup's head. Because harbor seal pups look so much alike, the tag will help identify the orphan as the one from Maine. The tag will come off later, all by itself, when the pup sheds his hair, just as a dog does every year. But for now, he looks as if he's wearing a hat many sizes too small.

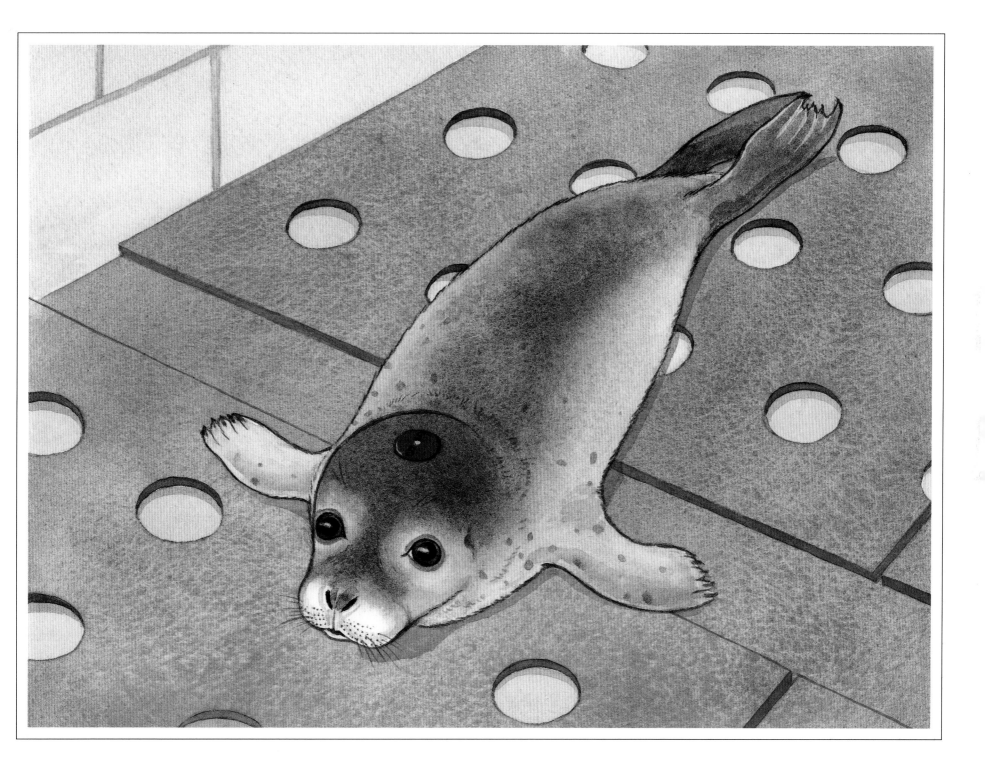

Before he can join the other pups, the newcomer must stay in a quarantine area. This is a separate room where the pup will live by himself until the aquarium staff is sure he is over his cold and won't give it to any of the other seals. The quarantine room is quiet and dimly lit. Here, sick animals can recover and new arrivals can get used to the smells, sounds, and activity of the center without having to deal with other animals right away. For now, the little seal likes the quiet—the way you do when you're home sick from school.

While he is in quarantine, the pup gets a name. The staff calls him "Howler" because of his very loud voice.

When the medicine makes his cold better, Howler is taken out of quarantine. He joins the other pups in a big, white room. Half of the room is a deep pool where they can swim. In the other half, there are platforms the pups can climb on and heat lamps they can sleep under. Two sliding glass doors open out onto the hallway.

The other pups sniff Howler to get to know him. They soon accept him into the little group.

Howler is snoozing under a lamp when another pup cries out. Startled, Howler looks up. Two volunteers, Lindy and Kevin, are at the door. They wear yellow raingear to keep dry. Lindy carries a towel. Kevin carries—lunch!

Soon all the pups are squawking to be fed. They are too young for fish, and ordinary milk will not give them the nourishment they need. Besides, cow's milk contains sugar, which seals can't digest. Trying to feed a pup the wrong things can make it sick.

So, the pups get a special meal. Years ago, after lots of tries, the aquarium staff learned how to make a formula like seal's milk. Trying to match the good nutrients in real seal's milk is a complicated process, and it takes two days to make a batch of formula. The result is a mixture of exact amounts of heavy cream, powdered cottage cheese, a variety of oils, and pre-prepared milk replacement. It looks like pancake batter. It smells like sour cream.

Howler is the first to be fed this time. Lindy picks him up and wraps him snugly in the towel, so only his head sticks out.

"Aaah-roooh! Aaaah-rooooh!" Howler complains.

Lindy gently opens the little seal's mouth and eases a soft, flexible tube down his throat. When the tube is in, Kevin pours formula into its funnel-shaped end. Howler closes his eyes and enjoys his meal. Each pup gets a little more than a quart of the formula every day, in four separate "meals."

Some pups drink from regular baby bottles, just like human infants. But most, like Howler, are fed through tubes because they don't understand that a bottle means "food." Besides, they're so sick when they arrive, there's not enough time for them to learn. The important thing is that they get fed!

When Howler is done eating, Lindy loosens the towel. His belly full, the seal pup wriggles across the floor and into the warm circle of light cast by a heat lamp. In a few minutes, he's sound asleep.

Howler spends most of his time sleeping, eating, playing in the water—and growing. He weighed only seventeen pounds when he came to the aquarium; he should have weighed twenty-five. The formula and the medicines he has been given have already helped him gain thirteen pounds. Howler has now been at the aquarium for three months, and it is time for something new.

After breakfast one morning, Belinda, another animal-care technician, comes into the room Howler shares with many other pups. She picks up Howler and carries him into another room. Here, there are other seals that are about Howler's size. On the floor of this room there are both a deep pool and a shallow tank.

In the afternoon, a volunteer named Robin lifts Howler into the cool water in the shallow tank. His whiskers tingle. Something in the tank is moving! He looks right, then left, and spots a tiny fish. Howler plows through the water after it. The fish is quick and small and gets away. Howler stops, looks left, then right. There it is! The chase is on again.

If Howler had stayed with his mother, she would be teaching him how to catch fish. Now, people need to help him learn to hunt. Over the next few weeks, Howler spends many hours in the shallow tank, chasing minnows, pinning them against the tank wall with his whiskery snout, and letting them wiggle free so the game can start again.

Eventually, he learns that fish aren't just for playing with; they're for eating. Howler is no longer fed the formula. Instead, he dives into the deep pool and catches the frozen fish that the staff thaws out and tosses to him and the other young seals.

Soon he will go home.

At six o'clock one rainy September morning, Greg Early enters the room where Howler and three other young seals are sleeping. He looks at Howler, who has now been at the aquarium for five months. The pup weighs forty pounds—the size of a healthy young harbor seal. He has learned how to feed himself. Greg knows Howler will be okay on his own, in the wild. Howler raises his head, blinks, and stretches. To him, today's just another day—so far.

In the hallway, Connie, Jim, and Belinda, all wearing waterproof parkas and rubber boots, are getting two carriers ready. One is made of wood and is painted blue. The other is plastic with a wire mesh door—like the carrier Howler arrived in, only bigger.

The blue wood carrier is brought into the room. It smells strange, and the seals are unsure of it. Two plop into the water, to watch the proceedings from a distance.

Jim stands between a female seal and the pool. Together he, Greg, Connie, and Belinda urge the female pup into the crate. The door is shut, and Belinda and Greg carry her out to the truck.

Now comes Howler's turn. He is not afraid. He trusts these people and knows they would never hurt him. With a little encouragement—a piece of mackerel tossed into the carrier—Howler clambers inside.

By truck, the aquarium staff will take Howler and the other young seal to the release site, a hundred miles away at the tip of Cape Cod. Greg drives carefully because the rain has made the roads slippery.

Howler is quiet. In his carrier, he listens to the hiss of the tires on the wet pavement and to the muffled voices of the people in the cab of the truck.

At the release site, the beach is empty and cold and drizzly. The aquarium people hunch their shoulders against the damp cold of early fall and lift Howler's carrier out of the truck. He will be released first. Each person takes a corner of the carrier. They pick their way carefully out across the sand.

Howler peers through the wire door of the carrier. His nose brings him scents he has not smelled for months—the wind and sand and wild, foaming water. Suddenly, the wire door of his carrier swings open, and there is nothing between him and the sea.

Howler hesitates at first, but the lure of the ocean is strong. He wriggles out. The rain and chill do not bother him.

With a lurch he slips into the water. Moving quickly through the surf, Howler bobs in the swells, his big dark eyes wide as he looks back at the people on shore. Then he dives again, out of sight.

Greg, Connie, Jim, and Belinda watch for him. Minutes pass. Suddenly, Connie spies a gray spot against the blue-gray water.

"There he is!" she shouts.

Howler is out in open water.

He is on his way home.

GLOSSARY

Digest: how the stomach changes food so the body can use it

Hypodermic: what your doctor uses when he gives you a shot

Microscope: a device that makes small objects look larger

Nourishment: food

Nutrients: the parts of food, like vitamins, that keep the body healthy

Parasites: tiny animals that live inside and get their food from the bodies of bigger animals

Pneumonia: a disease that makes the lungs swell and fill with fluid

Quarantine: separating a sick person or animal from others to prevent the spread of sickness

Replacement: an object that is used instead of something else

Species: the scientific group to which an animal belongs

Stethoscope: a tool that lets a doctor listen to a patient's heart and lungs

Technician: a person who is specially trained to do a particular job

Veterinarian: a doctor who takes care of animals